THE SNEAKY SUB

ZAC MARKS

Cover Model: Ryan Watts

Ryan won a photo competition to appear on the front cover!

"There is no need to run all the time. I know what to do and I wait for my moment."

Lionel Messi

1. PROBLEM

'I win again!' Luke throws down his controller and performs a crazy dance, wriggling his butt in my face.

'Only because you cheated!' I grin and push him away.

We've been playing for hours, our eyes glued to the screen. He hasn't won every game, but he usually comes out on top. That's hardly surprising; I can't afford a console like this, so I don't get to practice.

'There's nothing wrong with an occasional slide tackle, Jed!' He raises his hands comically. 'If your guys keep falling over, it's hardly my fault!'

'Yeah, unlucky, Jed,' chips in Brandon, ruffling my hair.

'The ref was blind. Let's go again.'

'We don't have time,' says Luke. 'We have to leave soon.'

I glance at the clock. He's right. 'Sure, ok. Then you better get ready.'

He opens up a drawer and pulls out his shin pads and

football socks. He sits on the bed and starts tugging them on. I've been wearing my orange Foxes kit all morning and Brandon probably slept in his, so we're both set to go.

'I hate putting these on,' he moans, pulling a face, and we both laugh.

I love spending time with Luke. He moved to the village a few months back, and we've become close friends. His dad is the local police sergeant as well as our new coach. Everything is working out amazingly well.

There's just one problem: Luke and I play in the same position. We both like to be centre-forward, and there's only room for one of us on the team.

Don't get me wrong: I'd be happy to play out on the wing, but Rex and Brandon have those covered. Rex is unbelievably skilful and there's no way any coach is going to leave him on the bench. That leaves me, Luke and Brandon fighting for the remaining two places. None of us wants to watch from the sidelines.

And to make it worse, we have the same problem at school. The three of us all have to compete for places alongside the ever-annoying Tristan.

It's tough having to battle it out.

We've talked about it and agreed that it won't get in the way of our friendship. We don't want to make things awkward.

But, honestly, things *are* awkward. We're all pushing ourselves at training, proving our worth. And we're hoping that our friends mess up, so we get picked instead.

'Do you need the loo?' Luke folds his socks down below the knee, making sure they're exactly right. I'm surprised he doesn't use a ruler. 'You don't want to have to use the ones at the pitch!'

'Good point.' I head to the bathroom. He has a nice house, but it's not posh. When I go to Brandon's, everything is expensive and spotless and I can't relax. This place is more like Dave's; when I visit, I feel at home.

I force myself to go, then splash some water on my face and check my hair. I know I'll play well, as long as I get picked. I just have to hope that I don't spend most of the game on the bench.

When I get downstairs, Luke is holding my boot-bag.

'Here,' he says. 'Don't forget this. For a moment, I was tempted to hide it.'

I smile at him. 'You're a funny boy. Don't worry. I'm sure you'll get to play.'

'I hope my dad lets me on for more than fifteen minutes this time.' Luke says it with a touch of bitterness in his voice, and I can relate. He has it harder than Brandon and me. Sergeant Brillin has been super-careful not to show any favouritism. As a result, Luke ends up on the bench more than anyone else.

We fill up our water bottles at the sink.

'Ah, good, you're ready!' Sergeant Brillin walks into the kitchen in a tracksuit which looks a size too small. 'Think we'll win this one, boys?'

'Of course!' I say. 'We're on fire.'

'I'm glad you're confident, but let's not get ahead of ourselves. I'm told that Tuckford are a good team.'

'They're pretty decent,' agrees Brandon. 'We drew last time we played.'

'I see. Where do you think you went wrong?' The sergeant sounds like he's interviewing a suspect.

Brandon shrugs. 'Dunno. They were lucky, I guess.'

Luke's dad isn't impressed. He was probably hoping for something more insightful, but you're never going to get that from Brandon.

'We weren't as fit as we are now,' I point out. 'That should make a difference.'

That reassures him. He nods. 'We'll find out soon enough. Let's get moving.'

We all stuff our feet in our sliders and get into the car.

Today is an away game, and I'm glad. We're going to get wet enough in the drizzle without having to contend with ankle-deep mud at our own field. They cancelled the match at school yesterday at the last minute because of the weather. I hope today's game doesn't get called off as well.

It only takes twenty minutes to drive to Tuckford. As soon as we arrive in the small car park, we clamber out of the car, eager to get moving.

'Do you mind giving me a hand with the stuff, Jed?' asks the sergeant as he opens up the back.

'Course not,' I say, grabbing the heavy bag full of equipment.

We trudge over to the pitch. Tuckford have a nice setup. There are changing rooms and there's even a small hut where parents can buy tea. On the far side of the field, the other team are running drills.

A few of our guys have arrived, but we're not great at getting to matches early. I'm relieved to see Dave is here. He couldn't join us for our early morning gaming session because he had to go to his sister's tennis tournament.

'You made it then?' I say, walking over to him.

'Just about,' he replies. 'But our car was making the weirdest noise. One day, it's going to give up completely. It's only a matter of time.'

I shiver in the cold drizzle, then jog on the spot to stay warm. 'I hope I get to stay on the pitch today.'

Dave glances around to make sure Luke and Brandon aren't in earshot. 'You should do, mate. You're better than either of them. But don't get big-headed about it.'

I smile at him, reassured. There's a reason he's my best mate. 'Do you think we'll win?'

Dave looks over to where Tuckford are practicing. 'It's a tough one. They're a tight unit. But I haven't seen much magic.'

I know exactly what he means. Good discipline and basic skills only get you so far on the pitch. You need something else as well. That's something the Foxes have in spades.

'Speaking of magic, here's Rex,' I say, as the brand-new BMW arrives in the car park, looking out of place next to Sergeant Brillin's battered hatchback.

'About time,' says Dave. 'We kick off in ten minutes. Hadn't you better put your boots on?'

I nod and sit down on a wet bench. The dampness soaks through my shorts as I open my bag.

I love my new boots. They're a size too big, but I bought them like that so I don't grow out of them any time soon. I wear two pairs of socks to compensate.

But something feels weird as I pull them out. Someone has knotted the laces together, not just once but loads of times, making it impossible to pull the boots apart.

'What on earth...?' I scrabble with the knots. 'Someone's tied my boots together!'

'Who would do that?' Dave shakes his head in disbelief.

'That's bad, Jed.'

He's right. It's hopeless: I'll never get them undone.

Brandon and Luke are chatting at the edge of the pitch. Luke is laughing as if they have some kind of private joke. But surely they couldn't have...?

If either of them had done it, they wouldn't have told the other one. But it must have been one of them. I've been at Luke's house for hours. They could have slipped down and sabotaged my boots while they went for a toilet break or something.

'Here, let me try.' Dave can see I'm getting nowhere. He takes them and tries to pick them apart. He gets one knot loose, but there are way too many and they've been pulled stupidly tight.

Sergeant Brillin calls us over. I'm holding on to my useless boots, blinking back tears.

'It's nearly time for kick-off,' says the sergeant, not noticing the state I'm in. 'Jed, Brandon, you're starting with the others. Luke, you're gonna be...'

'On the bench, as usual,' sighs Luke. 'I know.'

The sergeant ignores him, but he suddenly notices what's in my hands. 'Come on, Jed. Get your boots on. There's no time to mess around.'

'I can't. Someone's tied them together.' I lift them up to show him. 'I'm never gonna get all these knots undone.'

'Oh, crikey,' says Sergeant Brillin, taking them off me. 'They've made quite a job of it as well.'

He gets distracted as the ref beckons us. The other team are in position. 'Ok, Luke, it looks like you'll have to start while we sort Jed's boots out. Good luck, lads.'

I stand there, wet and angry, while everyone else files on to the pitch. A few minutes later, the ref blows his whistle and they're off. I watch jealously as Brandon and Luke race forward with the ball.

They're playing well, but I should be out there, not them.

One of them has betrayed me.

I intend to find out who.

2. WET

'We're going to need some scissors.' Dave's dad inspects the boots carefully. 'These laces are done for. Best to cut them off and start again.'

I nod. 'Sure. Do whatever you need to.'

Sergeant Brillin had to focus on the game, so I was relieved when Mr Hughes offered to help. We're standing at the edge of the pitch and I feel thoroughly miserable. We've been trying to sort the boots out for ages. Even my feet are wet: I wasn't planning to wear sliders for long. Now I don't have anything else and my socks are exposed to the rain.

'The thing is,' adds Dave's dad, 'I'm not sure if I have any scissors with me. I'll check in the car.' He jogs off.

While I wait, I watch the match. I'm annoyed to see that Luke and Brandon are playing well. I should be pleased; they're my friends and of course I want the Foxes to win.

But seeing them together, knowing that one of them is responsible for this, I kind of wish they were making a mess of it so the team would want me to come on. Instead, I watch as Luke skilfully backheels the ball to Brandon, who powers it into the back of the net.

1-0 to the Foxes. We're winning!

And I couldn't feel worse.

'I'm afraid I don't have any,' says Dave's dad as he returns. 'I thought there were some in the glove box, but they're not there.'

Just my luck.

'So, what do we do?' I ask. I know I sound desperate. That's because I am.

'I'll see if Sergeant Brillin has any.' Dave's dad heads off to ask, but comes back shaking his head. 'Sorry, Jed. We're going to have to give up for now.'

'Ok. Thanks anyway.' I try not to sound mad at him. It's not his fault. He's only trying to help.

I huddle on the wet bench, wishing I'd brought my coat. I thought I'd be warm enough because I'm usually running around. My teeth are chattering as I watch my team having fun. Dave keeps glancing at me, worry etched on his face. At half-time, he runs over.

'Couldn't my dad sort it?' he asks.

'Yeah. He sorted it. I just thought I'd sit here and enjoy the nice weather.' I shouldn't be having a go at him, but I'm too angry to care.

'Mate, that sucks. I'd let you have my boots, but they're way too big.'

'Thanks.' I'm smaller than most of my teammates, so no-one is going to be able to swap. Not that they'd want to.

'Who do you think did it?' asks Dave.

'I've been with Luke and Brandon all morning. It has to be one of them. I took my boots to Luke's house before the match.'

'I don't believe they'd do something like that.' Dave likes to believe the best about people.

'Well, they did. So much for us being mates.'

'Look, don't jump to conclusions and don't make any accusations. There might be another explanation. Give us time to work this out, ok?'

'I guess.'

My head knows he's talking sense, but it's not like I can turn my emotions off, is it? One of my closest friends has betrayed me and, because of them, I've missed the match and won't get to play. It's not fair and I'm fuming.

I want to slip away, to get out of there before I do or say something stupid. I can't, though. Sergeant Brillin brought me here and we're over ten miles from my house. I can't walk that far in the rain but the thought of getting back in the same car as Luke and Brandon makes me feel sick.

I sidle up to Dave's dad, the only person who's likely to help. 'Any chance I can get a lift back with you?'

'Sure, don't see why not.' He looks at me with sympathy. 'Not having a good day, are you?'

'Not really,' I admit. 'I hate everyone right now.'

'Not me, I hope?' He grins. 'Want to come back to ours after the match for a bit?'

'I'd love to, but I'm drenched.'

'You can borrow some of Dave's clothes. They'll be too big, but alright for dossing around the house. He won't mind.'

'Great. If you're sure?'

'Yeah, it's fine. It'll do you good.'

He's not wrong. I need a friend right now. And Dave is the only guy I can actually trust.

We're quiet for a moment as we watch the game. Brandon has the ball and chips it over a defender, so it lands neatly at Luke's feet. This time, Luke gets the glory as he wrong-foots the goalkeeper and slips it in the bottom corner.

2-0.

Maybe the team don't need me.

Dave's dad sees the depressed look on my face and holds out his keys. 'You must be cold. Want to sit in the car?'

'That would be awesome. Thanks.' I jog over and climb

in the back of the old grey people carrier. I lean back on a worn seat and consider everything that's happened, glad to be out of the rain.

I can't see the pitch from here, but that's ok. I'm too worked up to see Brandon and Luke score any more goals. I need time to calm down.

I also need to work out which of them is to blame.

And to figure out what I should do.

***

Things seem a million times better after I've had a hot shower at Dave's and put on one of his old tracksuits. It's so big on me, I look like a rapper, but I don't care: I'm warm and dry.

Being here with Dave and his family is a better way to spend the afternoon than going back to my place while Mum is at work. We're sitting on the floor of Dave's room throwing a pair of balled up socks to one another. It's something we always do when we chat.

'It's more likely to be Brandon,' he says. 'He's the practical joker of the two. He probably did it as a funny prank. He'll have no idea how angry you are about it.'

'Possibly.' Dave's right that Brandon is the mischievous one. 'But Luke usually ends up on the bench. He has more motive.'

'He wouldn't do it. He's a mate. And he's not devious like that. He's a straight-up guy.'

'Maybe that's what he wants us to think?'

We pause our game as someone knocks and Dave's dad sticks his head around the door.

'Everyone feeling better?' he asks.

'Yeah. A lot,' I admit, with a smile. 'Thanks.'

'Dave, why don't you find some scissors so Jed can free his boots. Hunt out an old pair of yours and strip the laces out of them so he has something to replace them with.'

'Sure.' Dave gets up and gives me a cheeky smile. 'Or perhaps Katie has some pink laces we could borrow?'

I jump up and raise my fist playfully. 'Don't even think about it!'

He laughs and we make our way down the stairs.

'Wait a minute,' he says. 'What about Luke's sister? Was she in the house? She might have done it as a joke on her brother's mates?'

'Nah, I wondered about that.' I sigh, sadly. 'But she was out all morning at a friend's house. So it was just us and Luke's parents. And I don't think Sergeant Brillin did it, do you?'

'No. Anyway, he'd use handcuffs!'

I give Dave a playful punch. He fends me off and grabs

some scissors from the kitchen. Together, we snip the laces out of the knotted boots, pulling them free.

'We keep my old boots in the garage,' he says. We wander through. There's three pairs on the shelf. But the thing is, they're all bright colours and my boots are black.

'Maybe I *should* ask Katie if she's got some laces,' I say. 'They might be less crazy than these.' I pick up a battered neon-green pair which pretty much glow in the dark.

'I don't have any black ones,' admits Dave. 'But you can have any of these that you want.'

'Those are probably best.' I point to the yellow ones.

'Yeah, ok. Here, you do one and I'll do the other.' He picks up a boot and starts pulling out the laces. I do the same. Once we've finished, we head back to his room to re-thread my boots. It's depressing: the yellow laces make them look cheap and nasty.

'Any idea how much black laces would cost?' I ask.

'A few quid, I guess.' Dave says it dismissively, like it's no big deal. For me, that's still a lot of money. 'I'm sure you'll be able to get some soon.'

'Yeah. Probs.'

'Brandon might have some?' suggests Dave.

'I'm not speaking to him right now.' I say it stubbornly, and Dave picks up on my tone.

'You can't be like that, Jed. For one thing, you don't

know it was him. It's not fair to blank him if he had nothing to do with it. The same's true for Luke. And we all play for the same team, so you have to stay friends.'

I stay silent. He's right, but how do you stay friends with someone who's betrayed you? And how do I know who I can trust?

'Make an effort, ok?' urges Dave. 'Whoever did it probably feels really guilty right now. They won't do it again. You mark my words.'

'I guess.' I don't want to be mad at my mates. But as I hold up the black-and-yellow boot, I know one thing for sure: every time I wear these, I'm going to be reminded of what happened.

And I can't just let it go.

3. TRAPPED

It's Monday and things are awkward as we get the bus to school. Brandon and Luke climb the steps behind me.

'Are you ok?' asks Luke, seeing I'm quieter than usual.

'No, I'm not,' I admit. I decide to be straight-up with them. 'Someone properly ruined my boots on Saturday so I didn't get to play, and I know it was one of you.'

'It wasn't me,' said Luke. 'I don't know anything about it, honest!' He looks offended that I'd even suggest it.

Brandon's sitting on the seat opposite. He raises his hands. 'Not guilty, mate. I mean, if I'd done that, I would only have done a few loose knots for a laugh. What they did was serious.'

I stare at them, perplexed. I want to believe them, but one of them is lying. 'Well, *someone* did it. And now I have to play football in *these*.' I pull out my boots and show them the yellow laces.

'Aw, mate, that sucks.' Luke is horrified. 'We have to get you some new laces.'

'Yeah, I probably have some at home,' says Brandon. 'Why don't you come to mine after school?'

'Maybe.' I don't know how I feel about that. 'But we have a football match, remember?' Our school team have a home game, and that means we'll be back late.

'After that, then.' Brandon shrugs. 'It won't take long.'

***

I spend the entire day at school guarding my boots. I don't want anyone tying them in knots before the game, so I can't let them out of my sight. I carry my boot-bag through the lunch hall, even though you're meant to leave all your stuff on the coat pegs. Every time I go to the toilet, I take them. No-one is going to sabotage these boots today, that's for sure.

When I get to the changing rooms, I feel positive. There's no rain today, just clouds. It's the perfect day for a match.

'Nice boots, Jed.' I'm standing up, pulling on my shirt, when Tristan approaches from behind. I turn around to face him. 'Only you could ruin a nice pair like that.'

'Ignore him,' says Luke, who's sitting next to me. 'He's trying to wind you up.'

Luke's right. I don't say anything, just pull on my shin

pads. I notice Luke has picked up his own boots and is stripping out the black laces.

'What are you doing?' I ask, curious.

'Giving these to you,' he says. 'You want black laces. Have mine. I don't mind the yellow ones.'

Is he saying that because he's a good friend, or because he feels guilty about what he did?

'Are you sure?' I can't believe he's offering.

'Completely. You want to swap?'

'Definitely. Thanks.' Whatever his motives, I'm not complaining.

We go as fast as we can, but re-threading the boots takes a while. It's nearly time for the match and the other kids have already left.

'I'll see you outside,' says Luke, when he's ready. His boots look stupid now, but he's acting like he doesn't care.

'Sure. I'm almost done.' I only have a few holes to go.

Luke's only gone for a few minutes before he pops back in. 'Coach asked if you could bring the corner flags with you when you come. The store is open.'

'No worries. But can't you take them?'

'I have to get the spare bag of balls.'

'Got ya.' He's got the harder job by far. Hauling those is not fun.

I stand up and check myself. I pull the socks over my

knees—the final touch. I'm set to go.

The equipment store is a brick-built shed right next to the gym. I head outside into the chilly November air and make my way towards it. The door is ajar and I step inside. It has a distinct smell: a mixture of dirt and football gear. The floor is covered in dried mud and the place is stuffed with sports equipment of every type. Hockey sticks fill a bin in one corner. Goalposts lean against a wall. The shelves are full of cricket stumps, plastic cones and training bibs.

Now, where are the corner flags? I glance around but can't see them. They must be here somewhere. I step forward to look behind some netball posts.

Without warning, the door slams shut and I hear a bolt being drawn across.

'Hey, I'm in here!' I shout. I run over and bang with my fist. 'LET ME OUT!'

Silence.

Everyone will be on the pitch by now, ready to play. They'll never hear me.

I try the door several times. I even try to barge it open, but it's heavy wood and won't budge.

There are no windows, only a dim bulb. I hunt around, wondering if there's anything I can use to escape, but it's no use.

I'm going to have to wait it out. Hopefully someone will come looking for the corner flags and find me. They must realise that I haven't shown up.

But the minutes tick by and no-one comes to my rescue. I realise that there are no corner flags in here after all. Someone has already taken them, so there's no reason to come back. Not until the end of the match, anyway.

I slide down onto the dusty floor and hug my legs for warmth. At least I'm out of the wind this time, but wherever I lean, something digs into my back. I grab some training bibs to sit on. That helps, but they smell weird, like they haven't been washed for a year. I try to push it to the back of my mind.

Time drags. I can't believe I'm stuck in a gloomy store cupboard, missing all the action, but there's nothing I can do.

At least I now know who the sneaky sub is. It has to be Luke. He's the one that sent me in here, waiting around the corner for the opportunity to lock me in. Which means he only offered me his laces to slow me down, to make sure I was the last to leave the changing rooms so his cunning plan would work.

So, surely it's Luke? Unless he and Brandon are in it together?

Either way, Luke is going to pay.

***

It's the longest hour of my life.

I'm cold and angry and still trying to plot my revenge when I hear movement outside. There's a scuffling and someone draws back the bolt. The door opens and Luke peers in.

'So you finally decided to let me out?' I demand, jumping to my feet.

'Jed! Why are you in here?'

I push him hard and he lands on the grass, looking shocked. 'You KNOW why I'm in here. You locked me in.'

'I have no idea what you're on about. I didn't do it, I swear.'

'You told me to fetch the corner flags.'

'That's right. Then I grabbed the balls and headed to the game.' Luke tries to get up, but I push him back down. 'Hey, pack it in!'

'And you didn't think to come and find me when I didn't show?'

'Brandon did. He ran back to the changing room, but you weren't there. He figured you must have gone to the loo. By the time I got to the pitch, the match was starting and Mr Davidson told us you'd come when you were ready and we should focus on the game.'

So, it could have been Brandon. But, then again, I was probably already locked in the store by then.

'So, who brought the corner flags?'

'No idea, but someone had already taken them. We guessed you'd realise that and come and join us.'

For a moment I doubt myself. Is it possible someone else is responsible?

'Jed, I'd never do this.' Luke looks up at me with a hurt expression, like a kicked puppy. 'We're mates aren't we?'

'Yeah, but I know how badly you want to play.'

'Not *that* badly.'

I want to believe him, I really do. But I'm not sure I can. Either way, his mum is giving me a lift home, so we need a temporary truce. I offer him my hand and help him up. 'Sorry,' I say, 'but you have to admit, it looks suspicious. And you'd be angry too if you'd spent the last hour in this dump.' I thumb towards the equipment store.

'True. That must have been grim.'

We walk back to the changing rooms, an awkward silence between us. Neither of us bother to get changed. I haven't even played football and Luke plans to shower at home. We grab our stuff and head to the car park where Luke's mum is waiting.

'How was the match?' she asks, smiling.

'I wouldn't know,' I say, bitterly. 'You'll have to ask Luke.'

4. BUS

I can't sleep.

Things are churning over and over in my head. I'm still not sure whether to believe Luke or whether he's pulling a fast one.

Was it really him who locked me in the store?

Or could it be Brandon?

I'm confused and angry. I toss and turn, my duvet getting rucked up in weird places. How can I protect myself if I don't even know who my enemy is?

And just as importantly, how do I get revenge?

By morning, I feel terrible. I have dark bags under my eyes as I slope down the stairs.

'What's with you?' asks Mum, grabbing her keys from the side.

'Couldn't sleep.' There's no point trying to explain. She has to dash off to work. Sure enough, a few seconds later, she's gone.

I grab a chipped bowl from the cupboard and pour in

some cornflakes, but there's hardly any milk. I slump down at the table and crunch my way through breakfast, the table wobbling every time I move.

What do I do?

I've already missed two matches thanks to someone sabotaging me. They can't get another chance.

Whoever it is doesn't want me to play football, that much is for sure. Whether it's for the Foxes or for school, they're trying to keep me out of their way.

I wonder if they'll try to stop me making it to the practice tonight. The Foxes always train on Tuesdays and Thursdays at 4.30pm and Sergeant Brillin always says that if you don't train, you don't play. I have to be there, whatever it takes.

Thankfully, I can leave all my kit at home and get ready here this time, so no-one will be able to mess with it. I just need to focus on making it to the next match.

I leave the house in plenty of time to catch the bus. I don't mind waiting longer than usual, and I don't need extra drama in my life right now.

Brandon and Luke are already at the stop.

'Hey,' says Luke, not sure whether he'll get a response.

'Alright?' I respond, sounding as friendly as I can.

'You're talking to us then?' asks Brandon. 'Luke told me what happened.'

'Sure. Sorry I blamed you. I figure you're right. Someone else did it. Probably Tristan. He hates me.'

That's not what I really think, because Tristan wasn't even at the match where my boots got knotted. But I've worked something out. When the time comes for payback, it will be a lot easier if Brandon or Luke aren't expecting it. In the meantime, I'm hoping that staying close to them might also give me a clue which of them is really guilty.

We chat for a while about what happened at the game that I missed. Apparently our school played well, but we only drew. I'm relieved they didn't win without me.

The bus pulls up and I reach into my bag for my pass. I hunt around for a few minutes, wondering if I put it in a different compartment to usual, but then realise that it's gone. All the other kids have boarded, and the driver is getting impatient.

'Come on, lad. Have you got it or not?'

'I must have lost it. Can't you let me on?' I tip my books onto the pavement while I kneel down and double-check the empty backpack.

'You know the rules. The company won't let me. No pass, no ride. Sorry mate.' He's not going to wait any longer. The doors close and the bus drives off.

Someone has taken my pass.

My bag was in the changing rooms for the whole of the

31

match yesterday. Whoever locked me in the storeroom could have stolen it.

And now I'm stranded.

School is miles away and we have no car. There's only one option: I'll have to bike.

I curse as I realise I've underestimated the sneaky sub once again. By the time I've cycled back from school at the end of the day, I'll be shattered. Then I'll go straight to training. Chances are, I'll play badly. That means I'll be less likely to be picked.

Well, I'm fitter than they think. They're in for a shock. However many miles I've ridden, I'll play my heart out, and Coach won't be able to bench me again.

I jog to my house and grab my bike out of the shed. I've cycled to school a few times before, but as soon as I'm pedalling out of the village, I remember how long it takes to cover the distance. I have to push myself if I'm going to make it there before the bell.

It's cold and the roads are wet, but thankfully it's not raining. Still, I'm soaked with sweat by the time I ride through the school gates.

I throw my bike into the rack, quickly securing it with my lock, then dash through the door seconds before registration. I made it. Just.

Brandon looks up as I walk in. 'Did you bike here?'

'Yeah,' I reply. 'Someone took my bus pass.'

'Mate, that sucks.'

He's right, but he has no idea how bad it *really* is. Brandon has never had to bike that far in his life. If he ever lost his pass, his parents would get him a taxi. Or maybe a private chauffeur.

'What is that smell?' Tristan mocks me as I walk past. 'Isn't it time for your monthly shower?'

I don't respond but a few others are laughing and my cheeks burn as I make my way to my seat.

***

I go through the whole day dreading the ride home, which is mostly uphill. I know that I'll be totally knackered but there's no way around it.

What makes the situation even worse is knowing that it'll take days to sort out a new bus pass. Weeks, even. The bus company aren't exactly efficient and there's probably an admin fee we can't afford.

Mum went mad last time I lost it. I don't even want to tell her, but I suppose I'll have to.

At home-time, I trudge outside, making my way to the bike rack. I watch the other kids walk by, heading for the bus, wishing I was going with them.

My battered old bike is waiting for me where I left it. At least no-one has nicked it. I half-expected someone to have taken that as well.

But as I undo the lock, I realise they've done something much worse. It makes me want to cry.

Another lock has been wrapped around my bike, securing it to the cycle rack. Someone has chained it up.

My heart is thudding in my chest. Football practice is in an hour, and our village is miles away.

But I can't take the bus and I can't use my bike.

I'll have to run.

I stuff my coat in my bag, take a deep breath and set off, my backpack bouncing on my shoulders. I run out of the school gates and down the street, trying to convince myself that I can do this.

But, truth be told, I'm already tired when I reach the edge of town. I slow down and check the time. It's gone 3.45pm and I've still got miles to go. The reality hits: I'm never going to make it to practice.

I guess the best thing would be to phone Sergeant Brillin to explain. Pausing at the roadside, I grab the phone out of my pocket and scroll down to his number.

The words 'NO CREDIT' flash up on the screen. I normally only use my phone with Wi-Fi. I can't call from here.

So, I'm going to miss practice and my coach won't even know why I'm not there.

The sneaky sub has well and truly struck again.

5. HOMEWORK

When I arrive in the village, the training session has just finished. I haven't had time to go home and change. Sergeant Brillin and Luke are collecting the cones.

I shuffle up to him in my school uniform. 'Sorry I missed practice, Coach.'

'Ah, Jed, I wondered what happened to you! I thought you never missed a session?'

'I don't. Well, this is the first one. Someone locked up my bike at school, so I had to run home.'

'All that way? Couldn't you get the bus?'

'I've lost my pass.' I decide not to accuse anyone yet. He is a policeman after all. 'I really want to play on Saturday. Please don't bench me because I missed training.'

He puts his hands on his hips and looks at me for a moment. 'Well, I'm sure we can let this one go. Just make sure you're here on Thursday, ok?'

'I will be.'

Luke has been listening in, and now he speaks up. 'How

are you gonna get to school tomorrow, Jed?'

'I dunno,' I admit. 'I haven't worked that out.'

'Want to borrow my bike?'

I don't, really. I don't want to take charity from the kid who might be sabotaging me at every opportunity. But he could be completely innocent. And I do need a bike. I'd been planning to borrow Dave's, but I'd been dreading asking him because I seem to use it more often than he does. 'Sure. That would be great.'

'You can come round now and pick it up if you like?'

'Thanks.'

As soon as all the equipment is stashed in the back, I climb into the car with them for the short drive to Luke's house.

'How long until you get a new bus pass?'

'Dunno. Next week if I'm lucky and if my mum can pay the admin fee. Otherwise I'll have to manage for the rest of term.'

'You can't bike in for a month! It's miles.'

I shrug. 'Don't have much choice.'

We enter his house through the back door and Luke kicks off his sliders in the kitchen. His mum is busy cooking dinner.

'Hi, Jed,' she says, warmly. 'Didn't you train today?'

I glance down at my tatty school uniform. 'Oh, err, no.

I had a problem with my bike. Luke's lending me his.'

'That's kind. But as soon as he's got that out for you, Luke has a lot of homework to do, so I'm afraid he can't play video games all night.'

Luke sighs. 'She's right. We have that English essay due in tomorrow.'

I groan. I haven't started it either. That's going to take all evening.

Luke takes me to the garage and wheels out his bike. 'Do you need a lock?' he asks.

I'm tempted to say 'yes', to see if he still has one, but I realise he probably has a spare.

'No, I've got mine. I'll try to get the caretaker to get the chain off tomorrow, so hopefully I won't need your bike for too long.'

'Keep it as long as you like.'

I'm surprised he's being this kind, but he might be doing this out of guilt. Or to throw me off the scent. I wish I could trust him.

'Thanks.'

I cycle home. My legs are already stiff after all the exercise today. They'll ache like crazy in the morning.

But before that, I have an English essay to write. And, worse still, I have to tell Mum about the missing bus pass.

It's going to be a long night.

***

You can always tell what mood Mum is in within the first three seconds. She's sitting on the sofa, a stack of unpaid bills on the coffee table. It doesn't look good.

'Hey, Mum.' I try to sound as upbeat as I can as I kick off my black trainers and slump down next to her.

'Hi Jed,' she says, glancing briefly at me. 'Did you have a good day?'

'Not great,' I admit.

'Well that makes two of us. I lost one of my clients today. They say they can't afford a cleaner any more.'

That's bad news. Every penny counts in our household. 'How many hours was that?'

'Three a week, but it all adds up. It's not easy finding work, especially in a small village like ours. We may need to tighten our belts.'

I can't remember a time where we didn't, but I don't point that out. We've never had much to live on.

'So, why was your day so terrible?' she asks, turning to face me.

'Someone stole my bus pass, so I had to bike to school.'

'Someone stole it or you lost it, Jed?'

I hate that about parents. They always jump to

39

conclusions and assume everything is your fault.

'Someone stole it,' I say, firmly.

'Why would someone do that? It has your picture on it. It's not like they can use it?'

I shrug. 'Dunno.'

She clearly thinks I've just been careless and dropped it somewhere. 'Do you know how much hassle it is to get a new one of those?'

'Yeah, I'm sorry, ok? I can't help it.'

'They charge a tenner just to do the paperwork.'

'Well, why don't you take it out of my pocket money. Oh, wait. I don't get any.' It's a low blow and I feel guilty the moment I say it.

She looks away for a moment. When she turns back, I can see tears in her eyes. 'I'm doing my best here, Jed. But we can't afford to pay for everything twice!'

I want to shout at her, to tell her how it's not fair, but seeing how upset she is so I draw close and give her a hug. 'It's ok, Mum. Don't worry about it. I'll bike in. It'll keep me fit for football.'

'It's a long way, Jed.'

Yeah, I know. I just ran it.

'Even better. My fitness level will be through the roof!' I try to sound enthusiastic.

'If you're sure.'

I'm not, but it's not like I have much choice.

'What's for dinner?' I ask, keen to change the subject.

'I don't know,' she sniffs. 'We've got nothing in. We're out of milk as well. Can you go and get us something with this?' Mum reaches in her pocket and pulls out some change. She deposits it in my hand. It isn't much.

'Sure. I'll find something.' I'm guessing that even going to the shop will feel like a marathon after the distance I've already covered, but I don't want to make her any more guilty. I slip my trainers on, grab Luke's bike and head off.

Living in a village you don't get loads of shops to choose from. There's only one, and it doesn't sell much. I find a plain cheese pizza that's on offer because it's nearly past its sell-by date, and some milk. The money just covers it, but there's none left for anything else. The pizza isn't that appealing but it's got to be better than another night of beans on toast.

By the time I get home, my legs are ready to drop off. I shove the pizza in the oven and make Mum a cup of tea.

She smiles at me. 'You're a good lad, Jed.'

'That's not what you said when I told you about the bus pass.'

She laughs and her face lights up. She ruffles my hair. 'Things are tough right now, but they will get better.'

'Yeah, I know,' I say, smiling back. 'But not for me

tonight. I've got stupid amounts of homework to do.'

Mum looks down at the pile of bills. 'You and me both, kiddo.'

***

My homework takes hours. Sometimes people say that but they actually did it in half an hour.

But I mean it *really* takes hours. Three hours and thirteen minutes to be exact. It's nearly ten by the time I'm finished. To be fair, I should have started this stuff weeks ago, but I always leave things to the last minute. Who doesn't?

I shuffle the sheets of paper proudly. It's the most writing I've ever managed in a day. It's not going to get me a great mark, but at least it's done. Mr Grierson is one of the strictest teachers in school. If you don't get stuff in on time, or hand in something shoddy, you're destined for a detention.

When I finally crash on my bed, I'm done in.

Today has not been a good day.

Tomorrow's not looking great either.

And unless I work out who's playing tricks on me, I have a feeling it's only going to get worse.

6. LOST

The thing about Wednesday is there's no football.

That normally makes it a dull day, but today I'm pretty relieved. I need a day for my legs to recover from the long run home. I already have to cycle to school and back: I don't want to do an hour on the pitch as well.

The other reason I'm glad is that I won't have to haul my football kit around, guarding it every minute of the day. Today, no-one can tie knots in my boots or steal my shorts or anything else, so I can relax.

At least, that's what I'm stupid enough to think.

I leave my bag by the coat pegs as I head off to lunch. But whoever's setting out to destroy me, they're pretty bright. They're always three steps ahead.

I don't realise what they've done until I get to English, and Mr Grierson asks for our homework. I scrabble around in my bag. It's not there and I start to panic, pulling everything out, bit by bit, looking for my masterpiece.

'Well, when I asked you to analyse Shakespeare, lad, I

wasn't expecting you to put on your own performance.'
Mr Grierson is standing over me. I can smell his breath: a
queasy mix of tuna and stale coffee.

'Sir?' I glance at him, confused.

'Do you think that if you act like you've lost your
homework, I'll believe you actually did it?' He raises his
eyebrows.

'No, sir. I mean, yes, sir. I did do it.' A few of the other
students are sniggering behind me, enjoying the show. 'I
spent hours on it last night.'

'So, in that case, where is it?'

'I don't know. It should be right here.' I gesture to the
pile of ruffled books and papers on the table. 'I think
someone took it.'

'Yes, I imagine they did.' Mr Grierson looks around.
Everyone is listening now, enjoying my misfortune. 'I
imagine that it was such an incredible piece of writing they
thought it would be worth a lot of money? Perhaps they
plan to get it published under their own name? Is that it,
do you think?'

He's mocking me, and I'm hot and flustered. 'No, sir.'

'So, why, boy, would anyone would want to steal your
below-average analysis of Shakespearean verse?'

'I don't know, sir.' I mumble it, my eyes focused on the
desk.

'Neither do I, lad. So, we'll find a time for you to repeat the exercise.'

'You're giving me detention?' My heart sinks.

'Yes, tomorrow after school.'

Tomorrow is Thursday, the next Foxes practice.

'I can't do that, sir. I've got football!' I look up at him, my eyes pleading.

It's pointless trying to negotiate. He's the sort of teacher who wants you to really suffer. As far as he's concerned, I deserve to miss football. He probably thinks I deserve the cane as well, if it were legal. 'Oh dear. Well, maybe you'll think harder about the consequences next time you decide to play video games instead of doing your homework!'

He strides to the front of the class, his judgement final.

Someone has set me up. They've taken my homework, and by the time I've done detention and cycled home, I'll never make it to training.

Which means Coach will never let me play on Saturday.

***

'I don't want to talk about it.'

I'm lying to Dave, and he knows it. We've been friends for long enough. I got home in a foul mood, and he's phoned me for a chat. He wants to meet up.

'Ok,' he replies, 'but let's at least have a kickaround. You might as well play some football this week.'

'My legs hurt. You try biking that distance and see if you still want to play.'

'Come on, Jed. How about I let you go in goal and I'll do all the running?'

'How about *you* go in goal and you still do all the running?'

'Fine.' Only Dave would agree to that.

'I'll see you there.'

I tug on a football kit. I always do, even if I'm playing with a couple of mates. Just taking off my school uniform makes me feel better.

I grab Luke's bike and ride down to the field, glad to be out the house where I've spent the last half an hour sulking. When I get there, Dave's doing kick-ups.

'Keep it off the ground,' he says to me, as I drop the bike and walk towards him. He sends the ball sailing through the air.

I catch it on the top of my foot, neatly flicking it up, then send it back. Even as I do it, I find the weight of it reassuring. There's something solid and predictable about kicking a ball. It puts you back in control.

We play like that for a while, the rhythm of our game calming me down, before switching to shots on goal. Dave takes his place between the posts, even though the mud is so deep it nearly swallows his boots.

I line up for a penalty.

'Are you going to turn up to the detention?' Dave asks.

'Yeah, I'm not stupid.' I run forwards and take the shot. It's heading for the top-right corner. He jumps for it but misses. It's one to me. 'If I don't go, I'll get six more, or be suspended. It's not worth it.'

'True.' He jogs off after it, then returns and rolls the ball to me. 'Did you manage to speak to the caretaker? To get the lock cut off your bike?'

'He's away this week. He won't be back until Monday.'

'That sucks. So, any idea who's trying to destroy you?'

'It has to be Brandon or Luke.' The air is chilly tonight and I can see my breath as I speak. 'They want to get more game time so they're doing everything they can to stop me playing.'

I run and shoot, this time straight down the middle. Dave drops to his knees in the muck, but scoops the balls into his arms. As he stands up, his white socks are caked in mud. 'Hey, can you not make me dive in this! Mum's gonna go mental.'

I laugh, despite my depressed state. 'Miles wouldn't complain.'

'Tell that to my mum.' Dave throws the ball towards

me. 'Anyway, are you sure it's not Tristan who's sabotaging you. He hates you and also wants to play up front.'

'Yeah, at school. But the laces thing happened at our Foxes game against Tuckford, remember? He wasn't even there. And while he might want to keep me from the school team, why would he want me to miss our Foxes practice? It doesn't affect him.'

'Perhaps he doesn't want you to play at the weekend?' points out Dave. 'We've got a match against his team on Saturday.'

I'd forgotten that. Tristan's team, the Welbeck Warriors, are our main rivals. We hate them and they hate us. It's usually a blood-bath of shirt-pulling, fouls and late tackles. 'Maybe, but that still doesn't explain last week. I'd love to pin this on him but Tristan was miles away when my boots got tied.'

Dave shrugs. 'Fair point. But I don't believe Brandon or Luke could do it.'

I line up my next shot. This time I power it high, but I get the angle wrong and it bounces off the crossbar. I curse, annoyed. 'I didn't either, but all the evidence points at one of them.'

'Which one?'

I glance left, then right. Which way should I shoot? I

could be cruel and make him slide through the puddle, but Dave's a mate. I wouldn't do that to him. Or would I? Brandon's the kind of kid who would do that every time. He's as cheeky as they come. If this was just someone playing pranks, then he'd be the prime suspect for sure. But this is hardcore.

I aim for the inside of the post. Dave makes a brave attempt, and tries to get his fingers to it, but it doesn't stop it going in. 'Nice shot.'

'Cheers.'

'This pitch is the pits, though.' Dave clambers back to his feet, his side brown. 'How does Miles do this every week?'

'Three times a week,' I point out.

'So, who do you think it is?' asks Dave again.

'It's got to be Luke.' I force the words out, not wanting them to be true. 'He's proper clever. And whoever is doing this is a genius. An evil one, but a genius none the less.'

Dave stands dead centre, his feet apart, ready for the next shot. 'You need evidence. You have to be sure.'

'I know.' I'm frustrated, and boot the ball directly at him. He's not expecting it, and catches it against his stomach.

'Ooof! Don't get mad at me! I'm trying to help!'

'Sorry.' I run my hand through my hair. 'Didn't mean

to.'

'You should secretly check his bag. See if he has your bus pass. Then, you'll know.'

'That's not a bad idea,' I admit. 'But what if he's thrown it away?'

Dave bangs his gloves together. He shrugs. 'What if he hasn't?'

7. EVIDENCE

Dave's right.

I have my suspicions, but I have to be sure. So, after my detention, I pop over to Luke's.

I pretend I'm there to apologise to Sergeant Brillin for missing training, but secretly I'm hoping they invite me to stay.

For once, my luck is in.

'Got time for a few games?' Luke asks. He's still in his kit, mud streaked down his side, his face flushed.

'Yeah, sure, that'd be great.'

'Wait a second, young man,' cuts in his mum, who overhears. 'You still need to change and shower.'

'I'll do it super quick,' says Luke. 'Jed can wait in my room.'

To my delight, his mum agrees. 'Ok, but no games until you're clean.'

It couldn't be more perfect. I can check for my bus pass while he's in the bathroom.

We head to his room and he starts stripping off his kit, leaving it in a grubby pile on the floor. Luke's not shy, but I look away as he takes off his briefs and grabs a towel.

'I won't be long,' he says. 'There are some comics in the corner if you're interested.'

'Sure.' I wander over and pick one up.

As soon as he's left, I put it back down and listen out for the sound of the shower. Once I'm sure he's busy, I close the bedroom door and grab his schoolbag.

Carefully, I take everything out, one compartment at a time, checking for the missing pass. There's one in the front pocket but it turns out to be Luke's. There's no sign of mine and I'm not sure whether to be happy or frustrated.

I still don't know if Luke is guilty.

Just as I'm about to give up, I spot a small zip pocket that I haven't checked. What's more, it feels like there's a card in there. My heart beats fast as I pull it out.

It's my bus pass!

Luke has taken it.

He really is the sneaky sub!

He's the kid who's been sabotaging me for the last week, trying to prevent me from playing matches or getting to training. He's the one who locked me in the cupboard and made me bike to school.

And now he's going to pay.

I wonder whether to take the bus pass back: it's such a hassle having to bike every day. But the problem is, if I do that, Luke will know I'm on to him. He might check for it and notice it's gone. And even if not, he gets the same bus, so if I catch it tomorrow, he'll work it out. I guess I'll have to bike for a few days more.

He has to think we're still friends. That's important, if the plan's gonna work.

I slip the card back into his bag, and make sure I leave everything exactly as I found it, before turning back to the comics. A few minutes later, he walks through the door, wrapped in a towel.

'Find anything you like?' he says.

Yeah, a bus pass.

'This one's pretty decent,' I say, holding it up.

'You can borrow it if you like. Bring it back on Saturday. You still on for the sleepover?'

'Can't wait! It'll be awesome!'

I'm meant to be going back to his after the game, but that's not likely to happen after I get my revenge.

You see, what I'm planning to do could wreck our friendship.

Chances are, he'll never want to speak to me again.

***

Saturday afternoon.

I'm ready an hour early for the match against Welbeck. I've filled up my water bottle and packed my bag ready for the sleepover, even though I probably won't go. But there's one last thing I need.

The top drawer in our sideboard is full of weird stuff: light bulbs, screws, broken pens and keys that don't seem to fit any locks. There're also some old tools in there: a couple of screwdrivers and an old hammer. I don't need any of that. The thing I'm looking for is much smaller. I hunt around for ages. Then, to my relief, I find it.

A tube of superglue.

It's tiny, and at some point we used some of it already. I hope there's enough.

My phone buzzes on the side and I check the messages: 'Hi Jed. Our pitch is in a terrible state. We're going to play at Welbeck, an hour later than planned. I figure you'll need a lift so I'll pick you up at 2.40pm ready for kick-off at 3.00pm. Make sure you're ready. Coach. PS: This is my new number so add it to your contacts.'

I curse, annoyed that I have to wait even longer to enact my plan. The bonus is that if Luke is further from his house, then my revenge will be even more effective.

I watch TV for a bit, feeling restless, still not entirely sure whether I'm doing the right thing. I wish I could stay friends with Luke and I really want to go to his sleepover tonight. But I can't let him get away with all the stuff he's done.

He has to be taught a lesson.

***

My phone rings again. This time it's Dave.

'Mate, where are you?'

'I'm at home.'

'We're about to kick off! Don't you want to play?'

'Course I do. But the match is...' I trail off, realising how stupid I've been. Again. 'Are we playing here? In Ferndale?'

'Yeah, at two. Which is, like, right now! You know that! What's going on?'

'I'll explain later. I'm on my way.' I hang up and dash out of the back door with my bag. I grab Luke's bike and ride there as fast I can. Thankfully, it only takes a few minutes. When I arrive, the teams are already making their way on to the pitch.

I dump the bike and run towards Sergeant Brillin. 'I'm here,' I puff. 'Sorry I'm late!'

'What's with you, Jed?' he asks, glancing at me. 'A month ago you were so keen on football you'd do anything to play. Now you don't show up to training and turn up late to the most important game of the season!'

'Someone's playing tricks on me!' I explain, hoping he'll understand. 'They texted me, pretending to be you, and told me the match had been postponed!'

He rubs his chin for a moment, as if considering the possibility. 'Who would do something like that?'

Your son.

That's what I want to say, but I don't. It's too early to make accusations. 'I don't know. But they're making my life hell. Please let me play. You need me out there! And I didn't get any game time last week!'

'Fine. Get your boots on. Quick! Before I change my mind.'

I run over to the park bench at the side of the pitch, where the Foxes subs always sit. I pull the boots out of my bag but I also take out the superglue. Luke tried to get me to miss the match again, and now he has to pay.

A few minutes later, I'm done. I leave my stuff on the bench, leaving just enough room for someone to sit next to it.

Sergeant Brillin has called Luke off and he's heading over, looking downcast.

'For a moment there, I thought I might get a game,' he says.

'I'm sure he'll put you on in the second half,' I offer. 'Sorry, mate, but I have to get on the pitch. Enjoy the show!'

He nods and slumps down. I suppress a smile, wondering if my plan will work. Luke doesn't know it, but he just sat in the superglue. In a few minutes, he's going to be well and truly stuck to the bench.

I can't wait to see his face when he finds out.

8. UNDERWEAR

The Welbeck Warriors are massive. They're kitted out in black, and they hulk over us like giants. Tristan is there of course, along with his loyal henchmen, Bryant and George. He sneers at me as I jog into position. They're our enemies for a reason. The two teams are evenly matched: what they don't have in skill, they make up for in brute force.

The ref blows the whistle and they kick off. Their first few touches are classic Welbeck. They've barely passed the ball twice before one of them boots it hard at Dave's face, knocking him to the ground.

It's not a surprise. When you play the Warriors, you always get hurt. By the end of this game, we're gonna be beaten and bruised. That's all there is to it.

Dave recovers fast, but looks shaken. Two minutes later he's shoulder-barged back to the muddy ground.

'Did I say you could get up?' I hear Bryant mutter to him as he jogs past, a wicked grin on his face.

I run over and offer my hand, pulling Dave to his feet. 'You ok?' I ask.

'I guess,' he replies. 'But they're worse than usual!'

It's not long before I get my own taste of the action, when Tristan barges into me, knocking me flying. I face-plant in the dirt. I pound my fist into the ground in frustration. It was my first proper chance at a goal.

As I clamber to my knees, Tristan offers me his hand. I don't want to take it but the ref is watching, wanting to make sure there are no hard feelings.

As he pulls me up, he crushes my knuckles at the same time. 'Better luck next time,' he says.

'I won't need luck,' I spit back, pulling my hand away from his iron grip. 'We're gonna win this thing and you know it! That's why you're trying to take us down!'

'Whatever. We'll see.'

Around ten minutes later, I get my first chance to prove my point. Rex is racing up the wing, jumping over outstretched legs and spinning past clumsy defenders. That boy has style.

'Here you go, Jed!' he shouts, as he lifts the ball high into the air, sending it in my direction. He's got it spot on, lining it up perfectly for me to blast it into the net.

Thankfully, I don't mess it up. Everyone is watching as I make contact and send it into the top-right corner.

Bodies collide with me, and I think I'm about to be crushed by one of our opponents, but it's just Brandon and

Rex smothering me in celebration, their sweaty bodies pressed against mine.

'Great goal, Jed!'

'Yeah, well done mate!'

I shrug as if it's nothing. 'It was a great cross.'

As soon as they've let go, I lean down and pull my socks higher. My kit is proper muddy now, more brown than orange, but so what? We're winning.

I glance over to Luke who's still sitting on the bench. He's clapping politely.

And he still doesn't know about the glue!

I get my head back in the game. Welbeck aren't going to take a defeat lying down, and they lay into us harder than ever. Theo gets sandwiched between two players, leaving him gasping for breath. The ref still doesn't call it.

Brandon is the next target. George, one of Tristan's mates, hurtles into him like an express train, knocking him to the floor and landing on top.

Even the useless ref can't ignore that, but a yellow card and free kick hardly makes up for it. Brandon is properly limping as he gets to his feet.

Sergeant Brillin calls him over and they have a brief conversation. At the end of it, Brandon nods and starts walking over to the bench.

All of a sudden, my genius plan doesn't seem so great. I

hadn't really planned for anyone properly getting injured. We only have one sub, and if Luke isn't able to play, we'll be down to ten men.

But it's too late to do anything about that now.

Luke tries to stand up. There's a confused expression on his face. He realises something isn't right. It's like I'm watching in slow motion as he forces himself off the bench.

Then I hear it: the sound of fabric ripping. As Luke gets to his feet, his shorts tear in two, leaving him standing in his underwear. He might not be shy, but no boy wants to be seen on a football pitch in his tight blue briefs. He covers them with his hands, his face turning red.

Welbeck burst out laughing. Even some spectators are grinning from ear to ear.

'What on earth?' Sergeant Brillin jogs over to his son, completely bewildered. I head over as well, pretending to be just as concerned.

'Th-Th-They were stuck to the bench,' says Luke. A tear runs down his face and I feel uneasy. Then I remember everything he's put me through. He deserves this.

'Well, you can't play in your undies, son.' Sergeant Brillin says it matter-of-fact, as if Luke was planning to do that. 'How bad's your injury, Brandon?'

'I might have sprained my ankle.' I don't think he's exaggerating either. 'I can't go back on the pitch.'

'Well, then, I guess we'll have to play with ten men.' Sergeant Brillin sighs. He knows that if we do, we're going to lose.

'No, Coach. Don't do that.' Brandon looks up. 'Luke can have my shorts.'

For a moment, no-one can take it in. We're all shocked by the sacrifice that Brandon is willing to make.

The brave boy is already reaching down and slipping off his shorts, revealing a pair of red and yellow Y-fronts. It would be hard to imagine a worse pair of underwear, but it's like he doesn't care. Welbeck nudge each other and giggle.

'Nice pants!' shouts Bryant.

Brandon ignores them and hands the muddy shorts to Luke, who pulls them on, looking relieved. The shorts are too small for him, but even tight shorts are better than none.

Brandon stands there in his Y-fronts, like it's the most natural thing in the world.

He smiles and gives a little wave to the shocked spectators. 'You can get a photo if you like?' he shouts, planting his hands on his hips. Now they're embarrassed and look away.

There's no two ways about it: he's a legend.

It reminds me why the Foxes are such an amazing team.

Kids like Brandon will do anything for their mates. We stand by each other.

But as I think on that, I feel guilty. What kind of mate am I? I blew it. My little prank on Luke nearly backfired and lost us the match. I should have been thinking about the team, not about my personal vendetta and whether I got to play. But I'll have to wrestle with my conscience later. We have a match to finish.

The ref looks relieved to be able to restart the game.

Dave takes the free kick, sending a solid pass in my direction. I race up the field, staying close to the ball, but I can hear someone right behind me, and he's closing fast. I glance over my shoulder: it's Tristan.

There's no-one to pass to. I'm on my own and I have to take the shot. The goal mouth is straight ahead, the keeper trying to close the angle, moving through the giant puddle that stretches across the box. Tristan tries to swipe my back leg, but I'm expecting it and pull away. I strike the ball hard and slip it past the surprised goalie.

Two-nil.

Rex runs over and gives me a high-five. 'Great shot!' he says.

The Warriors don't seem very happy but before they can come at us again, the ref blows his whistle. It's half-time.

Dave, Luke and I jog over to check on Brandon. He's sat on the bench.

'You ok?' I ask.

'It's just a sprain. I need to rest it.' He shrugs. 'Mind you, I'm a bit chilly. Have you got a top I can wear?'

'Sure, help yourself.' I gesture at the bag. Then I glance down at his undies. 'And there are some trackies in there, if you want them.'

'Awesome.'

I wouldn't normally have a change of clothes with me, but I'd packed for the sleepover, so Brandon is in luck. I realise I probably should have offered earlier.

He gratefully unzips my bag and rummages around, pulling out my trackies. He'll probably get them dirty, but I don't mind. He's a mate, and he took one for the team. I'm more than happy to share my clothes with him.

But as he pulls out the sweatshirt, something drops to the floor. He picks it up.

'What's this?' he asks, confused.

But Luke has already seen it and knows exactly what it is.

The tube of superglue.

9. FIGHT

'IT WAS YOU! You glued my shorts to the bench!' Luke pushes me hard and I land on my butt in the wet grass.

'I—I—I...' The words stick in my throat. How can I explain what I've done? It doesn't matter: he doesn't give me a chance. He jumps on top of me, pinning me to the ground.

'I thought we were mates!' He yells it in my face. 'I've never been so embarrassed! Why would you do that?'

'You know why!' I spit back.

He looks shocked and it distracts him. I pull him to the side and for a few moments we're wrestling each other one way then the other, rolling around like pigs in the mud.

And boy, is it muddy. I've told you about our pitch, right? It's basically a swamp, with more dirt than grass, even in the summer. Now it's November, it's a miracle they let us play here at all.

'What are you talking—' Luke doesn't finish his sentence as I force his face in a puddle.

He squirms away, spitting out grass before punching

me in the stomach. I'm winded, but swing my fist, catching him on the cheek.

'Lads, what's going on?' Sergeant Brillin is running over. He grabs hold of Luke and drags him away. 'Calm down, son! What on earth are you fighting about?'

'He stuck me to the bench!' Luke glares at me and I wonder if we'll ever be friends again.

'Is that true, Jed?' The sergeant looks shocked.

I want to deny it, but I'm not great at lying and they've already found the glue. I climb to my feet, caked in mud.

'Yeah. I did. So what?'

'So what?' The coach looks like he's going to explode. 'SO WHAT? Are you a few cards short of a full deck? What is wrong with you, lad?'

'I knew you'd take his side,' I say, sullenly. 'He is your son, after all.'

'I'm not taking sides!' Sergeant Brillin is clutching Luke's shirt by the neck. 'I just want to know why you'd do a thing like that.'

'Why don't you ask him?' I demand.

A crowd is gathering now. Tristan, Bryant and George are there, smirking at us, enjoying the show.

'Well?' The sergeant looks at Luke and shakes him slightly. 'Spit it out. What's he on about?'

Luke shakes his head, close to tears. 'I have no idea, Dad.

He's gone mental.'

'You stole my bus pass!' I blurt it out all at once and it's good to say it out loud. 'I had to cycle in for days, and I found it in your bag!'

'Is that true?' Sergeant Brillin's face is hard. He looks into Luke's eyes.

'No, Dad. He's lying. I never touched his bus pass. Why would I?'

'Check his bag yourself!' I say. 'As soon as you get in. You'll see I'm telling the truth!'

'Oh, I will,' says Sergeant Brillin. 'I certainly will.'

Luke gulps. He's afraid, alright.

'And he locked me in a store cupboard at school,' I add. 'And he tied knots in my laces!'

'You're crazy!' insists Luke. 'I didn't do any of that!'

'We'll deal with all of this later.' The coach straightens up and lets go of his son's shirt. 'You boys get yourselves a drink. And don't you dare start fighting again, you hear me?'

We both nod, embarrassed.

'Show's over, everyone,' says the sergeant, as casually as he can. 'Just a little misunderstanding, that's all.'

But it's not a misunderstanding.

Luke hates me, and I hate him.

The problem is, it's time for the second half, and we're

meant to be working together. As soon as the ref blows the whistle, it's clear that's not going to happen.

He runs up the wing with the ball, and I stay level with him, heading towards the box. There's a moment when he could pass it, but he doesn't. Instead, he tries to shoot. The angle is narrow, and it bounces off the post and back into the field, straight to the feet of a Welbeck defender.

I catch his eye but don't say anything. We both know how this is going to work. It's like we're on different teams. Neither of us will pass to the other. We're too angry.

Sergeant Brillin is watching, one hand over his mouth, shaking his head in frustration. He can see the problem too.

'Come on, boys, work together!' he shouts.

But you don't. Not when you're at war.

We might get away with it, if it was just us. But the whole team are affected. The Foxes are like a family, and when one of us is upset, it impacts everyone else. Our midfield have fallen to pieces and our defence is a shambles. Even Miles can't focus.

Welbeck come at us like an invading army. They take advantage of every mis-kick, every slow turn. It's a different game to the one we were playing before half-time and they know it.

They advance up the field, tearing holes in our defence.

I drop to my knees as they descend on the goal, overwhelming Miles with sheer numbers. It's no surprise when they score.

And that's only the first.

They come at us again and again, pushing and shoving, sliding and pulling, intercepting our sloppy passes and punishing us for the tiniest errors.

I want to cry as they score the second. And the third.

Now they're in the lead and they're not going to stop.

If Luke and I don't start working together, we'll lose this thing for sure.

I only get one more opportunity. I'm powering up the field, having shaken off my mark. The goal is dead ahead, but the keeper is right in front of me. I reckon I can take him, but if I'm honest, Luke has the better angle. He's off to the left and all it would take is a quick pass.

I want to, but I can't.

I won't be the first to back down.

He doesn't deserve to score.

I press on, taking on the goalie. It's a mistake. The lad has faster reactions than I expect. He sticks out his foot at the last moment, deflecting my shot harmlessly to the side.

I head towards the corner, expecting to take it, but Rex intervenes. 'Not today, Jed. Your head's not in this.'

Normally I'd argue, but I know he's right.

I jog back to the box, ignoring Luke who's behind me.

When Rex sends it curving towards us both, we're so focused on getting to it, we collide with each other and end up on the ground.

'You boys sure like rolling in the mud,' smirks Tristan, as we try to get up.

Neither of us say sorry. We ignore one another and press on.

Not that there's anything else for us to do. The ball is back at the other end of the pitch. Two seconds later, it's in our net.

Four-two to Welbeck.

That's how the game ends.

We lose.

Sometimes you walk off the pitch like a hero, with your team hugging you, celebrating the win. Other times you feel like a loser, disappointment etched on your face. But today is the first time I've shuffled off as a villain, my face bright red.

'Well, lads,' says Sergeant Brillin. 'I think the less said about that shoddy performance, the better, don't you?'

The boys murmur agreement. A few glance over at me and Luke. It's clear where the blame lies.

I grab my bag and go to pick up the bike.

'Where do you think you're going?' asks Sergeant

Brillin.

I turn around, confused. 'Home,' I say. 'I'm guessing the sleepover is cancelled.'

His next words come as a surprise: 'Oh no it's not. You boys have some stuff to work out. You're both coming with me!'

10. ENEMIES

'You can't make me!' I sound like a five-year-old, but I don't care.

'Is that right?' Sergeant Brillin stares me down. He's not used to being spoken to like that. 'Well, it's true that I can't force you to come back with us, Jed. But I promise you this: neither you nor Luke are playing any more matches with the Foxes until you sort this. So, if you walk off right now, you're off the team.'

'You can't do that!'

'I think you'll find I can.' He folds his arms, daring me to disagree. 'You boys have been firing accusations at each other worse than some of the guys I see down the station on a Friday night. We need to get to the bottom of this. And fast.'

I blink back tears. 'Fine.'

It's not fine, but what can I do?

'Right,' says the sergeant, 'you grab Luke's bike and meet us back at the house. Brandon, Dave, are you still up for a sleepover with these boys?'

'I guess,' says Brandon, looking a bit unsure. 'But I think I'll change and shower first.'

'Me too,' says Dave.

'Can you bring my trackies with you?' I say.

'Sure. You're gonna need them.' He grins at the state of my kit. He's not wrong.

'Can I at least go home and shower?' I ask the sergeant.

'No can do.' Sergeant Brillin shakes his head. 'I'm afraid we need to investigate the crime scene before anyone has the chance to tamper with it. You can get clean afterwards.'

Luke shuffles to the car with his dad. He looks more sad than angry. He must be aware he's about to get busted.

I set off on his bike, riding round to their house, wondering what's going to happen. The chances are, we'll both be punished. Me for gluing Luke's shorts. Him for everything else. But at least everyone will get what they deserve.

I pull up, wondering what kind of welcome to expect.

'Put the bike around the back.' Sergeant Brillin directs me through the gate.

I kick off my boots and pad into the kitchen, my socks leaving sweaty footprints on the tiled floor. Luke is sat at the dining table, feet apart, arms folded, like he's been told to sit down and shut up.

'Right, come on, both of you.' Sergeant Brillin leads the

way upstairs into Luke's room. 'Now, where's this bus pass?'

'In his bag, in that little zip pocket on the side. Unless he's taken it out.'

Luke doesn't say anything. He leans against the doorpost and gives me a dark look.

His dad grabs the backpack and checks it. I'm relieved when he pulls out the pass. Now he knows I'm not lying!

'Both of you have some explaining to do.' He raises his eyebrows. 'First, how did this end up in your bag, Luke? And second, how did you know where it was, Jed, if you didn't put it there yourself?'

The story comes out in pieces. I stand awkwardly in the middle of the room, describing how I got locked in a cupboard after school, and the way my homework magically disappeared so I'd miss the next Foxes practice.

Luke tries to interject, but his dad cuts him off.

'You'll get your turn in a moment,' says the sergeant.

I carry on with my account: I get it all off my chest, everything that's happened. By the end, even Luke looks shocked.

'Right, your turn,' says Sergeant Brillin, turning to his son. 'Is he right about this? Is this all your doing?'

'No, Dad! I'd never do any of that!' He looks hurt now, tears running down his face. 'Jed's a friend. At least, I thought he was. I don't know who did it, but it wasn't me!'

'So, explain the bus pass,' sighs the sergeant. 'How did that get there?'

'No idea,' admits Luke. 'But couldn't someone have planted it? To try to frame me?'

'Seriously? That's your explanation?' I say it with venom. I've been waiting to see him get nailed. He's not going to slip out of it now.

'It is possible,' allows the sergeant. 'You see, Jed, Luke doesn't lie. There are a lot of things he's not very good at. Tidying this room for one.' The man glances around, disapprovingly. 'But he does always tell the truth. And I can spot a lie a mile off.'

'But how... what...?' I can't form my next question. My brain is working overtime, and I'm realising how dumb I've been. I want to sit down, but I figure I'm too muddy to touch anything, so I just shift from one foot to another.

If Luke really is telling the truth, I glued him to a bench for no reason.

'I can't make you believe him,' says Sergeant Brillin. 'But until you boys work out your differences, you're both stuck in here and there's gonna be no gaming and no Wi-Fi. But first, Luke, you need to go and take a shower.'

'I'm not leaving him in my room again. Not like this. He'll put glue on my chair or something!'

'I won't.'

'If you keep on at each other like that, it's going to be a really long and miserable night.' Sergeant Brillin shrugs. 'You need to work it out.' Then, he leaves.

We stand there in silence for a few moments, red-faced. Luke looks up. 'Honestly, Jed, I didn't do it. It wasn't me.'

I stay quiet.

'Look,' he adds, 'I can see why you thought it was. And I get why you glued me to the bench. I'm not mad at you any more.' He walks over and puts a hand on my shoulder.

I pull away. 'I'm not sure I trust you,' I admit.

Luke nods, sadly. He sits down on a chair and pulls off his muddy socks. 'Ok, I get that. But you're a mate, Jed. I don't want that to change. Just tell me what I need to do to convince you and I'll do it.'

'That's fair.' My voice is strained.

'Right now, I'm going to take a shower.' Luke stands up. 'And I'll leave you in here, so if you want to take revenge on me for something I didn't do, then you can. I won't even tell my dad, I promise. Do whatever you want, if it makes you feel better. I just want us to be friends.'

He heads off to the bathroom leaving me standing there, confused. I walk over to the chair and slump down. It's only plastic, so it'll wipe clean, and I'm exhausted. I need time to think.

He sounds so genuine. I'm finding it hard to believe this is an act. I realise that if Luke had taken the bus pass, surely he'd have thrown it away or hidden it somewhere else as soon as he got home. He wasn't likely to forget he had it stashed in his bag.

But if Luke is innocent, then someone else planted it in his backpack. They could easily have done that. Luke's stuff was right next to mine in the changing rooms. They must have known I'd find it eventually, or perhaps they thought I'd have time to report it missing and Mr Davidson would carry out a search and Luke would get into trouble.

I should have figured it out sooner.

So, if it really isn't Luke, then who is the sneaky sub?

Who has been doing all this stuff to me?

There's only one other suspect: Brandon.

And he's going to be here any moment now.

11. HOSTAGE

The front door slams and I hear him padding up the stairs.

Luke is still in the shower, so I'm alone when Brandon walks into the room, dressed in the latest Villa kit, socks pulled up to his knees. He always wears football kit, except when he's at school, so it doesn't really come as a surprise.

'Hey, Jed.' He opens his bag and pulls out my trackies and hoody. 'There you go mate. Thanks for the borrow.'

'No worries.' I pull them on, glad to cover up the mud. Now I can relax without worrying about getting everything in the room dirty.

'So, what's happening? Did you and Luke make up?' He settles down on the floor, his back to the wall.

I look at him, trying to work out if he's really capable of the stuff I've had to deal with. 'We're getting there. But if Luke didn't do all that stuff to me, there's only one person who could have.'

'Oh yeah?' Brandon looks interested. 'Who's that?'

'You.' I advance towards him, like a lion stalking its prey.

He looks nervous, but doesn't get up. He knows it would be pointless trying to run. There's nowhere to go. 'Hey, back up! It wasn't me!'

'You sure about that?' I pounce on him, grabbing his arm and twisting it around so he's forced face-down on the carpet. Brandon and I are both small for our age, but he's rich and spoilt and nowhere near as tough.

'Let me go,' he says.

'Not until you confess!' I push his arm further up his back and he cries out. He's getting loud, so I grab Luke's muddy football sock and stuff it in his mouth. It's disgusting, soaked through with sweat and mud. I can smell it from where I'm sitting.

'I want to hear it from you,' I say. 'I need closure on this, Brandon. We've been mates for years. Did you sabotage my stuff so I wouldn't get to play for school or the Foxes?'

He shakes his head vigorously and tries to say something but it comes out muffled.

'I'm going to take this out now,' I tell him. 'But if you try to shout for Sergeant Brillin, then you're gonna be eating it for a very long time, do you understand?'

He nods, his eyes wide.

I pull the makeshift gag from his mouth, and he pulls a face of total disgust. 'Awww, man. That's gross! Don't put that back in.'

Realising I now have the perfect weapon to torture him with, I hold the sock close to his face. 'What, this? You better start talking. Did you lock me in the store at school?'

'What? No, of course not!'

'That's not a great start.' I push the sock right against his nose and he squirms beneath me, trying to pull his head away.

'Let's try again,' I say. 'Did you steal my bus pass and put it in Luke's bag?'

'No! Jed, I don't do stuff like that!'

'Wrong answer. How about my homework? Did you take it out of my bag so I'd get in trouble with Mr Grierson?'

'What homework? I'm not even in your English class! Please don't put it in my mouth! I'm telling the truth!'

'I don't believe you.' I hold his nose so he opens his mouth, then force the sock in. The expression on his face would be comical if the stakes weren't so high.

I'm distracted as the door opens behind me and Luke wanders in, a towel wrapped around his waist.

'Jed, what are you doing?' It's a bit of a pointless question, really. He can see perfectly well.

'I'm getting Brandon to confess. If you didn't mess with my stuff, it must have been him.'

'Is that one of my socks?' Luke looks worried. 'You

can't do that to him, mate. That's grim.'

I shrug. 'He deserves it. Anyway, I'll stop as soon as he owns up.'

'But what if it wasn't him?' Luke pulls some clothes out of the drawer. 'What if you're wrong again?'

'Well, who else could it be?' I say. 'Only you and Brandon play up front. And Rex, but he doesn't go to our school.'

'Yeah, but Tristan does.'

Brandon makes a muffled noise, but I ignore him, holding the sock in place. 'Tristan doesn't play for the Foxes and he wasn't there the day my laces got knotted.'

Brandon tries to speak again. This time, I have pity on him and remove the sock.

'I've worked out what happened! I know how he did it!'

'How *who* did it?'

'Tristan!' Brandon looks excited. 'Luke's right! Tristan did it all! Let me explain.'

'Ok, but this better be good.'

'Yeah, yeah, fine. But listen! Tristan doesn't want you playing for the school team, right? Especially since Luke arrived, and it means he might get subbed.'

'True.'

'So he's been trying to stop you. That week when your laces got knotted, we were meant to be playing against

Kirton Academy after school on Friday, remember?'

'Yeah, but it was cancelled because of the weather.'

'Right, well maybe Tristan had knotted your boots earlier in the day, before the match was called off. He knew that if you couldn't use them, you couldn't play. He could easily have done it at break-time.'

'And because we didn't play, you didn't have any reason to take them out of the boot-bag until Saturday, when you were playing for the Foxes.' Luke realises what Brandon's trying to say. 'Is that possible, Jed?'

'I guess.' I hadn't stopped to consider it before, but I never checked my boots on Saturday morning before I set out.

'And then, on Tuesday at school,' says Brandon, 'Tristan was there when Mr Davidson asked Luke to fetch the balls and to tell you to get the corner flags. He must have followed him to the changing rooms.'

'So he waited until I'd gone, then he grabbed the flags and hid around the corner so he could lock you in?' Luke looks relieved as he says it. We have an explanation that makes sense.

'But what about making me miss practice?' I point out. 'Why would he do that?'

'He didn't want you playing at the weekend, when we took on his team.' Brandon is still struggling for breath under the weight of my body. I get up, and let him scramble free. 'He knew you were one of the biggest threats, apart from Rex, but he couldn't do anything to Rex because he doesn't even go to our school.'

'So he tried to stop me getting to practice.' I can't believe I didn't figure it out before. 'He stole my bus pass, and locked up my bike so I'd have to run. He knew I wouldn't make it back.'

'Then he stole your homework, so you'd get a detention,' added Brandon. 'It's pretty genius, really.'

'And he put the pass in Luke's bag hoping we would fall out, or Luke would also get into trouble.' I sigh and lean against the wall. 'And it worked. Because we fought, we lost to Welbeck.'

'The thing I don't get,' said Luke, 'is that you told me that someone texted you before the match, trying to get you to miss it or show up late.'

'Yeah.'

'Well, how would Tristan get your number?'

I stare at the floor. Now it's my turn to confess. 'We used to be friends.'

Luke looks shocked. 'You and Tristan?'

'I thought he was cool when I first started at school. But then I realised what an idiot he is, so we properly fell out.'

'And by then he already had your number?'

'Yeah, it's not like I've ever upgraded my phone.' I glance over at Brandon, apologetically. 'Sorry, mate. Looks like I shouldn't have accused you either. Are we good?'

'Sure.' He gives me a mischievous smile. 'I'll forgive you. But first you have to spend a minute with this in your mouth.'

He holds up the filthy orange sock.

'You can't be serious.'

'I'm afraid so.'

'It's only fair, Jed,' agrees Luke. 'You did just torture him for no reason.'

'Really?' I look at it with disgust.

'Really.'

Tentatively, I take the sock and lift it closer to my face. It smells revolting. 'It's not hygienic. What if I get ill or something?'

'That didn't stop you from doing it to me.'

There doesn't seem to be any way out of this. Not if I want to rescue our friendship.

'If I do this, then we're even, right?' I need to check it's worth it.

'You do this, and we'll call it quits,' agrees Brandon.

What choice do I have? I open my mouth wide and push in one end of the sock, the end that has been on Luke's foot for the last few hours while he played football.

I won't tell you what it tastes like, because I don't want to think about it. Needless to say, it's rank.

'Ok, I've started the timer.' Brandon is properly enjoying this now. He perches on Luke's bed, a wide grin on his face.

At that moment, Dave arrives. He's somewhat surprised to walk in and find me standing there with Luke's dirty sock hanging from my mouth. 'Am I interrupting something?'

'Jed had some penance to do,' explains Luke. 'Don't worry. In one minute, we're all gonna be mates again.'

The thought of that cheers me up; it makes even the foul taste worthwhile. The minute seems to take forever. Eventually, Brandon declares that it's up.

I spit out the sock and wipe my mouth in disgust. 'That was a long minute!'

Brandon grins. 'It might have been two!'

I decide not to make anything of it. That's just Brandon. Besides, I probably deserve it.

While I go to the bathroom to rinse out my mouth, the others explain to Dave what we've worked out.

'I told you,' he says, looking smug. 'I said that neither Luke nor Brandon would do anything like that.'

'Yeah, yeah, whatever.' I give him a weak smile. 'What do you want? A medal saying "I told you so"?'

'That'd be nice.'

'So what do we do now?' Luke looks around.

'We take revenge,' I say, determined.

'That didn't go so well for you the last time,' points out Dave. 'We could just let it go.'

'Never! Tristan has to pay!'

'We could play some tricks on him,' says Brandon. 'How about we put superglue on his shin pads so he has to wear them for a week?'

I shudder at the thought. 'That's hardcore. But it also sounds dangerous and we could get into serious trouble.'

'What, then?' Brandon looks around, seeing if the others have any ideas.

'I think I've got it,' says Dave. 'I've worked out exactly how we can teach Tristan a lesson he'll never forget.'

***

When Sergeant Brillin pops in to check on us, he's surprised to find us all laughing and joking together.

'Looks like you boys have worked out your differences,' he observes.

'Yeah, sorry Coach.' I shrug. 'It was my fault. I was wrong. Someone framed Luke.'

'I'm glad to hear you say that, Jed,' he says, warmly. 'Do

you know who did it?'

'We have some idea,' I say. 'But don't worry. It wasn't one of the Foxes, we're all good. Thanks for making me come round to sort it.'

That seems to satisfy him. He smiles and nods. 'Well, you could at least open a window! It smells like something died in here! Luke, get that filthy kit into the laundry basket before it makes its own way there!'

12. REVENGE

The school cloakroom is packed full of bags and coats. It's also deserted: everyone has headed off to lunch, abandoning their stuff.

Dave and I have been hiding in the corner for ages.

'What if he doesn't come?' I whisper. The plan we came up with seemed so clever, but now it doesn't look like it's going to work.

'He'll come.' Dave is matter-of-fact. 'It's his only chance to sabotage your kit before practice. He's just getting lunch first.'

'I wish we were,' I mutter, my stomach grumbling.

'You can eat afterwards.'

'That's easy for you to say. You have a packed lunch. I get a free school meal, and they stop serving at half-past.'

'Shh.' Dave puts up his hand and I clam up.

Someone is coming.

I peer between the coats and see Tristan wandering through the cloakroom, hunting for my bag. Dave pulls out his phone and starts recording.

We've deliberately made it easy to find. I mean, it's an old battered light-blue Man City backpack with graffiti on—it's not hard to spot. But we've left it dead centre. We don't want Tristan to have to work too hard or he might find us instead. Sure enough, he soon sees what he's after.

Checking no-one is around, he unzips it. Then he pulls something out of his blazer pocket. It takes me a moment to work out what it is.

It's a small bottle of golden syrup. He pops off the cap and twists it upside down, about to pour it over my school books and football kit.

'That's far enough, Tristan.' Dave's voice makes even me jump.

Tristan freezes and looks around. 'Who said that?'

We emerge from our hiding place, Dave holding his phone in front of him. 'Want to explain why you were about to fill Jed's bag with syrup?'

He panics. 'I wasn't. I mean, this isn't what it looks like. Can you please stop recording?'

'Sure.' Dave puts his phone away. 'But I think we need to have a chat, don't you?'

Tristan has turned bright red. He knows he's been caught red-handed. It's good to see the boy with the sharp haircut and chiselled features looking so flustered. 'You're not going to rat on me, are you?'

'That depends,' says Dave. He folds his arms and casually leans against the wall.

'On what?' Tristan sounds whiny now.

'Where's your bag, Tristan?'

'Over there.' He jerks his head towards the corner.

'Go fetch it.'

The bully shuffles over and grabs his top-brand schoolbag. He dumps it on the bench. 'There.'

'Open it up.' Dave is enjoying himself, but he knows we don't have long. A teacher could come at any moment. 'Quickly. Jed wants the key to the bike-lock.'

'Fine.' Tristan rummages around and throws me a key.

But Dave isn't finished. 'Take out your football boots.'

Tristan does as he's told. His Nexus Cheetah's still look brand new. I know what Dave is going to do, and it almost seems a shame.

'I think they need some syrup in them, don't you?'

Tristan looks like he's going to be sick. But he takes the bottle back out of his pocket. 'Seriously?'

'Deadly,' says Dave. 'Get a move on.'

Tristan squeezes the bottle into the boots, sticky syrup pouring down.

'That's enough,' says Dave, once the bottle is nearly empty. 'Don't use it all.'

Tristan looks up. 'Why?'

'Because you're going to need some for your pants. Just a small squeeze will be fine.'

'Please, you can't make me...' The look of fear on Tristan's face is a joy to see.

'Fine, don't do it,' Dave takes his phone back out. 'We'll just give this footage to the head and tell him about everything you've done.'

Tristan turns white. 'If I do it, you have to delete the footage,' he mumbles.

'If you do it, I hold on to the footage until I'm sure you're not going to sabotage any of our stuff again.' Dave's so confident, he almost scares me. 'But if you leave us alone, no-one else gets to see it, I promise.'

Tristan looks at the syrup in his hand and slowly lifts his shirt. His designer boxers are visible above his trousers and he pulls the waistband forwards. He takes hold of the bottle and squeezes it. A line of golden syrup drops into the gap and he pulls a face.

'That's good. Now some in the back,' orders Dave.

'But I've got to wear these all afternoon! And for football practice!'

'What's your point?' I ask.

I expect him to object, but he sighs and turns around so we can watch. He squeezes the bottle hard, the last of the syrup disappearing inside his boxers. It's not much, but it will be enough to make him uncomfortable.

'Happy?' he asks, a grimace on his face.

'Sure. Now don't you dare try to wash it off or tell anyone, else the deal's off.' I follow Dave out. As soon as we're clear, we burst out laughing and I give him a high-five.

'That was awesome!' I say. 'But that wasn't what we planned! I thought we were going to make him pour water on his kit?'

'Well, he brought the syrup,' grins Dave. 'It seemed a shame not to use it.'

***

Tristan is one of my classes that afternoon. He sits in front of me. Throughout the lesson, he's squirming in his seat.

I dread to think what it feels like: having sticky syrup in your pants. His face says it all: he looks like he's swallowed a wasp.

'Is something wrong, Tristan?' asks Mrs Kelworthy, getting distracted by his constant fidgeting. 'Do you need the toilet?'

'No, miss. I'm fine,' he says through gritted teeth.

'Well, sit still then.'

'Yes, miss.'

It's even better when we get to the changing room after school for football practice. Tristan has to peel off his trousers. There was more syrup than I thought and a few sticky streaks have made their way down his legs.

'What's that?' asks Bryant, who's getting changed next to him. 'What happened to you?'

'Shut it,' snaps Tristan.

I glance over as he pulls on his football kit, dragging shorts, shin pads and long socks over the sticky mess. He's sat on the bench, wiping his hands on his shirt.

He catches my eye. We both know what he needs to do next, and it gives me as much joy as it gives him pain.

He takes the boots out of his bag.

I wonder if he's cleaned them, but he won't have had much time. Besides, if he has, they'll still be wet and horrible.

It doesn't look like he's even tried.

He forces them on, one at a time, before tying the laces carefully, with a grim expression.

As we file out of the changing rooms, he falls in line next to me.

'Don't worry, Tristan,' I say, 'only an hour more to go. I hope you're not *too* uncomfortable.' I probably shouldn't bait him but it's too good an opportunity to pass up.

'I've kept my end of the deal,' he says. 'You have to

destroy the footage.'

'Sure,' I agree. 'As soon as we're sure you have no more tricks up your sleeve.'

He snorts through his nose and jogs out the gym.

'You realise he's going to want revenge?' says Dave. 'We're both gonna pay.'

'Yeah,' I say. 'But it's still worth it!'

And I'm right.

Playing football is always a joy. But knowing that Tristan has boots full of syrup makes it even better.

It's no surprise when he plays badly. He's hating every minute. All he wants to do is shower and change. But as he plays, sweat runs down his body, mixing with the sugary goo, making it worse.

When he jogs past, I'm sure I can hear a squelching noise coming from his boots. His shorts are sticking weirdly to his butt, and he keeps trying to pull them loose.

At the end of the game, Mr Davidson calls us over.

'Well, boys, that was a good game,' he says, 'for most of you, anyway.' He looks briefly at Tristan, who's staring at the ground. 'We've rescheduled the match against Kirton Academy for this Friday. Hopefully the weather will be better this week. I'll put the team-sheet up on the noticeboard tomorrow. Check for your name, and if you're on there, make sure you bring your kit and come prepared. Ok?'

'Yes, sir.'

'Great, go and get changed.'

***

When we find out the team the next day, Tristan hasn't even made it as a substitute. He mutters something under his breath and stalks off. I almost feel sorry for him, but then remember everything he did. He deserves to miss a game. More than one, in fact.

That means that me, Brandon and Luke are all able to play up-front in the starting line-up. Dave's on there as well, in his usual place in midfield.

'The three amigos!' says Brandon, hugging us both at the same time. 'Kirton Academy don't stand a chance!'

'Please don't call us that; it's a terrible nickname!' says Luke and Brandon laughs.

'It's so good that we can finally play a game without worrying about which of us is gonna get subbed,' I say. 'I wish it was always like that.'

'Don't worry, it will be.' Luke gives a half-hearted smile.

'What? Why?'

'I'm fed up with us falling out at the Foxes, Jed. I've decided to play in defence. I spoke to Dad about it last night.'

'Are you sure?' I couldn't dream of losing my place up front. I live to score goals.

'Completely. It doesn't mean as much to me as it does to you. Besides, I might get more game-time.'

'But someone will still need to be sub,' I point out. 'We have a full team as it is.'

'Yeah, but the defence isn't as strong. Anyway, I've told my dad I'll stay on the bench as much as he wants. I'm the newcomer. It's only fair. I don't want anything to get in the way of our friendship again.'

'Why? You worried I'm gonna glue you to a bench?' I punch him gently on the arm.

'No,' he says. 'I'm worried you're gonna make me eat a sock.'

We push and shove our way to lessons, laughing and joking as we go. I realise right then just how much it means to me: having friends like these.

I can't believe I nearly lost them.

For a while, I thought they'd betrayed me, that football had come between us.

But now I know it will never do that; it never has.

Football doesn't come between people.

It brings them together.

And I wouldn't swap these friends for anything; not

even for a contract at Man City.

Wait, on second thoughts: I might do it for that!

A NOTE FROM THE AUTHOR

Thanks for reading 'The Sneaky Sub'.

I hope you enjoyed it, and you're looking forward to hearing more stories about Jed and the Ferndale Foxes.

If you haven't read them yet, then make sure you get a copy of the other books in the series which are full of action, suspense and... you guessed it... football! They're available now on Amazon.

There are a few other things that might be of interest.

First, you can connect with my readers' club at:

www.subscribepage.io/footballkids

If you're under thirteen, your parents will need to sign up for you. I'll keep you informed of any new releases, as well as giving you opportunities to get freebies, prizes and giveaways.

Second, you can check out my Instagram account **@zacmarksauthor** where I post football forfeit challenges, where kids sometimes end up egged or with boots full of shaving foam! Check it out and get your parents to message me if you want a challenge of your own!

Finally, it would be a huge help to me if you would get your parents to post a review on Amazon for this book. Could you do that? I promise I read every review!

Stay connected – I love hearing from my readers, and who knows, maybe you or your team could make it into one of Jed's adventures!

Thanks so much for being a part of my story.

Zac.

THE CRAFTY COACH

The Ferndale Foxes are in trouble. With no coach, the team will fold.

Jed needs to act fast! He can't imagine life without football. But saving the team is going to be tough: he has to find a way to turn things around, both on and off the pitch.

There's one person who might be able to coach them, but he isn't the kind of person you'd usually ask. Will he be a great choice or will it end in disaster?

THE GROUNDED GOALIE

Every team needs a goalie. But what if he doesn't show?

Miles is missing and no-one knows why. Jed and his friends need to figure out what's going on. Will Miles ever be allowed to play again? If not, who's going to take his place? The Ferndale Foxes need to work as a team if they're going to solve the mystery.

But Jed is feeling the pressure. Will he ever get answers, or spend the whole season sliding through mud? And will he be able to save anything, let alone Miles?

THE TERRIBLE TOURNAMENT

It should be the best summer ever. But it's the worst!

When the Ferndale Foxes head off for a football tournament by the sea, they have no idea how tough it will be.

Jed and his teammates can't catch a break, and everything seems to go wrong. Faced with one problem after another, the team falls apart.

It's not easy to stay friends when you feel like a loser.

Will they be able to turn it around before it's too late?

THE PERILOUS PITCH

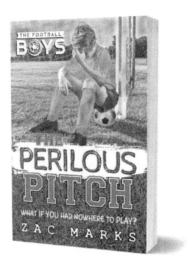

It's the worst pitch ever. But it's better than nothing.

Now, the council want to take it away.

When Jed and his friends hear there are plans to build on their pitch, they do everything they can to stop it from happening. It's their home ground, and there aren't any other places to play in the village.

But who's going to listen to a group of kids? And how can they make the council change their mind?

THE CHRISTMAS CUP

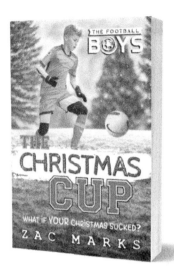

Everyone loves Christmas. Except Jed.

He has nothing to look forward to, the house is cold, and he can't afford any presents.

There is one good thing; his football team are taking part in the Christmas Cup. They're determined to win, but the odds are against them.

Will the Ferndale Foxes overcome the challenges that face them at every turn? Or will it all end in misery and disappointment?

DO YOU LOVE FOOTBALL?

Aged 9-13?

Do you eat, sleep and breathe football?

Would you like to take on a challenge?

Want to win some new kit or free books?

Or even appear in one of the books?

Visit **www.subscribepage.io/footballkids** for
information on all this and more!

Read on for a
sneak preview of
'The Grounded
Goalie'...

'Where is he?' says Dave, hugging himself to keep warm.

I can't answer. None of us can. No-one knows what's happened to Miles, and the game is about to start.

'If he doesn't show up soon, someone else will have to go in goal,' points out Rex, sounding worried.

It's a grey, overcast day and a light drizzle has started to fall. We're all desperate to get moving; no-one wants to stand around.

I glance at the pitch. It's in a state as usual, more mud than grass, even near the centre. A large puddle stretches from one side of the goal to the other.

'There's no way I'm diving in that.' Brandon folds his arms, daring us to contradict him.

We're all thinking the same. But if Miles doesn't show, one of us is going to get stupidly muddy.

Our coach—Sergeant Brillin—walks over. He's holding his phone. 'I'm afraid I have some bad news. Miles isn't able to play today.'

'Why not?' I ask. 'Is he injured?'

Sergeant Brillin looks flustered. 'I... err... I'm not sure, Jed... Let's not worry about Miles right now. We need to figure out who's going in goal.'

'Shotgun not me,' I say.

'You can't shotgun that!' says Dave. 'We need a fair way to decide.'

'What do you suggest?' asks Luke.

Dave always knows what to do. 'We all write our names on slips of paper. Then choose one at random.'

Brandon shrugs. 'Sounds alright.'

Dave jogs off to find some paper and a pen. The rain is getting worse. We're all thoroughly miserable by the time he gets back.

'Ok, let's get this over with,' mutters Rex.

Dave crouches down and scribbles out our names. He tears the paper into pieces, folding each one up small. He gathers them into his hands and stands up. 'Whoever has their name pulled out, they're in goal, ok?'

We nod, wondering who's going to suffer.

'Rex, you can pick.' Dave holds out his cupped hands.

Rex reaches forward and pulls out a slip. He unfolds it and I see him relax. It's clearly not him.

'Well, who is it?' says Luke, desperate to find out.

'Brandon.' Rex holds up the paper to show us.

'No way!' Brandon pulls a face and runs his hand through his hair. He turns and looks at the goal, then makes a noise of disgust.

'Afraid so. Fair's fair. You got picked.' Dave won't take no for an answer. 'Suck it up, rich boy.'

There's some good-natured banter as we all slap Brandon on the back and wish him luck. He looks like a kid who's about to visit the dentist.

'There are some spare goalie gloves in my dad's coaching bag,' says Luke.

'You need to change your top,' points out Rex, 'or put something over that shirt.'

'I'll grab my sweatshirt. At least it'll keep me warm.' Brandon jogs over to our pile of stuff and comes back with a brand-new drill top and some tatty gloves.

Meanwhile, Sergeant Brillin is chatting with the referee, explaining the reason for the delay.

The field is as bad as ever. The grass squelches underfoot and within minutes of the ref blowing the whistle, we're all spattered with mud. We have the worst pitch in the league. We probably have the worst pitch in the country. But I can't think about that. Right now, I have to focus.

The Brookland Beavers might sound like a terrible football team, but they're surprisingly good on the pitch.

We get a few quick attempts on goal, and things seem hopeful, but the defence soon sharpen up and close us down, making it hard to score. We can win this, but it's not going to be easy.

They soon get in a shot of their own, slicing the ball towards the bottom corner. Brandon hesitates, then dives. He's too late and the ball ends up in the net.

He climbs to his feet, his side plastered with mud. As he wipes his dirty gloves on his shirt, Dave jogs over to him. 'You need to react faster than that!'

'You try diving in this!' complains Brandon.

'I know it's tough,' agrees Dave, 'but let's face it, you're gonna be covered by the end of the match, so there's no point hesitating every time they take a shot. Brave it out like Miles would.'

'I have no idea how he does this every week,' says Brandon darkly. But he takes his place back in the goalmouth.

'This isn't going to go well,' mutters Dave as he jogs back up the pitch towards me. 'Brandon's a useless keeper.'

It's true. Brandon always plays up front. He doesn't enjoy being anywhere else on the pitch. He complains if he has to take a turn in goal.

'Best we can do is make sure they don't get too many shots,' I suggest. 'Then they can't score.'

It turns out that's easier said than done. In every game, both teams get *some* shots on goal. And if you have a terrible keeper, you soon pay the price. By the time the Beavers have scored their third, I'm beginning to realise how much we take Miles for granted.

Brandon is so muddy it's not even funny. He's been trying, I'll give him that. It's not really his fault. He's a great striker but a shocking goalie.

Sergeant Brillin has come to the same conclusion. He beckons me over.

'What's up, Coach?' I ask.

'Look, Jed, it's three-nil already, and it's not even half-time. If we leave Brandon in the net, then we're going to lose this match by double-digits. I need you to take his place.'

'Why me?' I feel my stomach tighten at the unfairness of it.

'Honestly?' Sergeant Brillin uses his no-nonsense voice, the one you can't argue with. 'Because, without Miles here, you're the best goalie we have. I've seen you in training. The team need you. What do you say?'

I groan. 'Do I have a choice?'

'Not if you want the Foxes to win.'

I'm silent for a moment, weighing up my options. 'Fine. I'll do it. But just this once.' I jog over to where Brandon is standing, shivering in the wind. 'I'm going in goal,' I say, unable to keep the annoyance out of my voice. 'Apparently you suck so bad that I have to take over.'

Brandon shrugs. He's not offended. 'Here, you'll need these.' He tugs off the gloves and drill top and throws them at me.

'Gee, thanks so much.' All the stuff is wet and slimy,

and I have to force myself to tug the shirt over my head. Then I strap on the gloves and step forward into the puddle, the only place I can stand if I want to have any hope of defending the net. My nice boots aren't going to keep my feet dry today; wet mud oozes over the sides. Even though I'm wearing two pairs of football socks, I feel it soaking through.

And the worst part is I'll have to dive in it.

It's only a matter of minutes before the opposition take another shot. By now, they've worked it out. They're aiming for the bottom left corner, which is grim, knowing that no goalie is going to be keen to land in that.

But unlike Brandon, I don't hesitate. I spring to the side like a cat hunting a mouse, the tips of my fingers deflecting the ball around the post. Then I feel it, freezing-cold muck soaking through my kit and splashing on my face. As I scramble to my feet, I realise how terrible this is going to be.

If we're gonna have any chance of winning, I'm gonna be rolling around in it for the rest of the match.

'Thanks, Miles,' I mutter under my breath, trying to wipe my face and only making it worse. 'Thanks a lot. You'd better have a decent excuse for not being here.'

But what if he's injured? What if he can't play for months?

There's no way I'm doing this again.

I need to get to the bottom of this, and fast. The Foxes need their goalie back.

And I need a hot shower.

The sooner, the better.

Will Jed ever find out what happened to Miles? Get your copy of 'The Grounded Goalie' to find out!

<u>AVAILABLE NOW ON AMAZON</u>

Printed in Great Britain
by Amazon

31729442R00067